Tadpoles

Over the Moon!

First published in 2006 by
Franklin Watts
338 Euston Road
London
NW1 3BH

Franklin Watts Australia
Hachette Children's Books
Level 17/207 Kent Street
Sydney
NSW 2000

A CIP catalogue record for this book is available
from the British Library.

ISBN (10) 0 7496 6887 3 (hbk)
ISBN (13) 978-0-7496-6887-7 (hbk)
ISBN (10) 0 7496 6897 0 (pbk)
ISBN (13) 978-0-7496-6897-6 (pbk)

Series Editor: Jackie Hamley
Series Advisor: Dr Hilary Minns
Series Designer: Peter Scoulding

Printed in China

For Molly, Zachary
and India with love – J.A.

For Lucas – H.R.

Over the Moon!

by Hilary Robinson

Illustrated by Jane Abbott

W

FRANKLIN WATTS

LONDON • SYDNEY

Hilary Robinson

"I have always liked watching the magical night sky, and I would love to be the first author to jump over the Moon!"

Jane Abbott

"The nursery rhyme that this story comes from is one of my children's favourites. I really like the ending in this story!"

The cow and the cat
looked up at the Moon,
shining high in the sky.

"Look!" said the cat.
"Let's jump over that!"

"Oh yes!" said the cow. "Let's try!"

8

The little dog laughed
at the cat and the cow.

10

They jumped ...

"Look!" said the cat.
"By the dish and
the spoon,

the Moon has
dropped out
of the sky!"

Then all that night
they sang out a tune.

"Tonight is the night
that the cow and
the cat ...

21

"... ran and jumped over the Moon!"

Notes for adults

TADPOLES is structured to provide support for newly independent readers. The stories may also be used by adults for sharing with young children.

Starting to read alone can be daunting. **TADPOLES** helps by providing visual support and repeating words and phrases. These books will both develop confidence and encourage reading and rereading for pleasure.

If you are reading this book with a child, here are a few suggestions:

1. Make reading fun! Choose a time to read when you and the child are relaxed and have time to share the story.

2. Talk about the story before you start reading. Look at the cover and the blurb. What might the story be about? Why might the child like it?

3. Encourage the child to reread the story, and to retell the story in their own words, using the illustrations to remind them what has happened.

4. Discuss the story and see if the child can relate it to their own experience, or perhaps compare it to another story they know.

5. Give praise! Remember that small mistakes need not always be corrected.

If you enjoyed this book, why not try another TADPOLES story?